With love to Zoe Kennedy, Gbenga Chesterman,
William Evans, and Alice Harvey, who all got
together for a change at Suzannah and
Lawrence's wedding—and helped to make
their wish come true
—I. W.

For Jemma and Daniel, with love
—T. B.

Margaret K. McElderry Books
An imprint of Simon & Schuster Children's Publishing Division
1230 Avenue of the Americas
New York, New York 10020

First published as *The Snow Friends* in Great Britain by Gullane Children's Books, London
First U.S. edition, 2002
10 9 8 7 6 5 4 3 2 1

Printed in China
Library of Congress Control Number: 2001090799
ISBN 0-689-84930-3

wish, change, friend

WRITTEN BY
IAN WHYBROW

ILLUSTRATED BY
TIPHANIE BEEKE

Margaret K. McElderry Books
New York London Toronto Sydney Singapore

Little Pig lived quietly on the edge of the woods, under a big oak tree.

Not many small pigs like reading, but Little Pig did.

He had plenty of acorns and twigs and books, and for a long time that was enough for him.

Then, one day, he
found three new
words in a book.

Wish was one.
That was easy.

The next was harder.
It was ***change***.

The last was hardest.
It was ***friend***.

wish

Little Pig closed his eyes and tried the words out.

"I ***wish*** for a ***change*** and a ***friend***," he said to himself.

The ***wish*** worked. It started to snow.
And that was a nice ***change***.

So Little Pig
took some acorns
and some twigs
and some snow.
And he made
a ***friend***.
"Let's go," said the
snow friend.

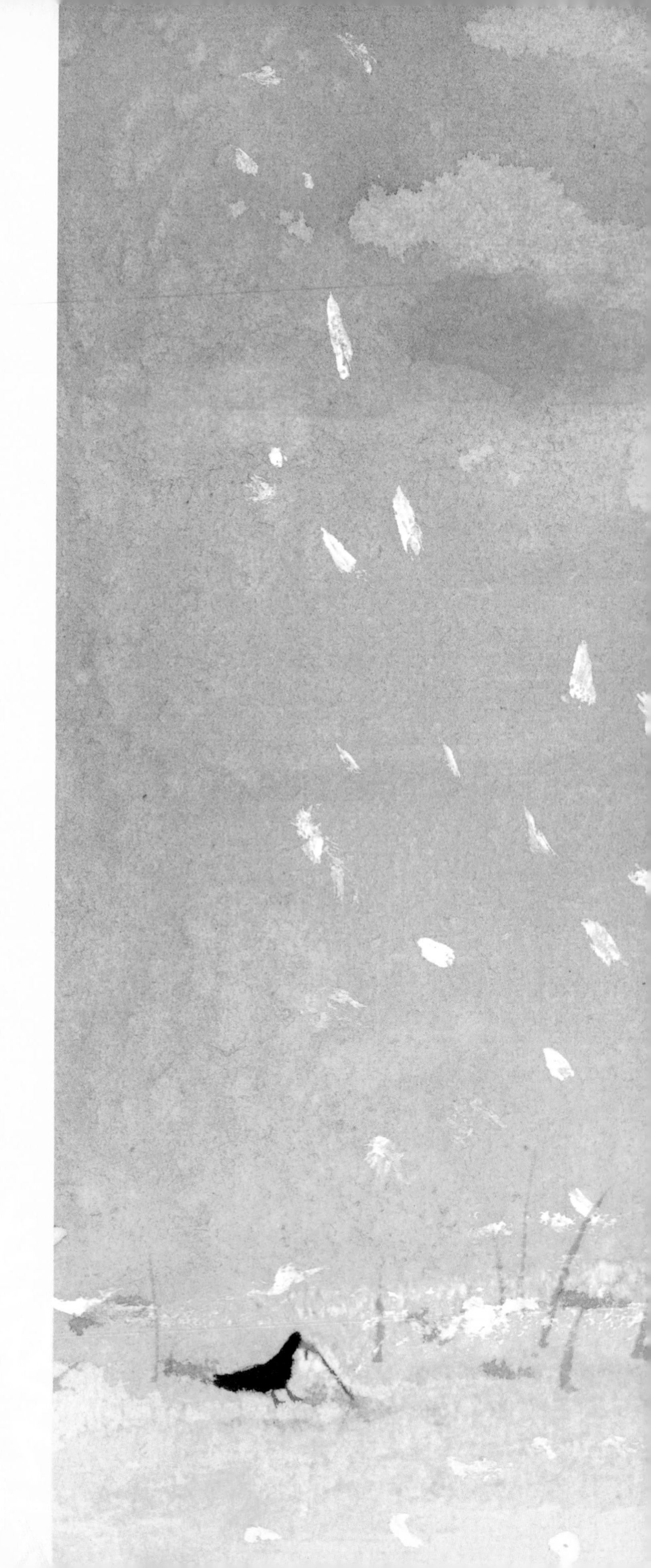

And off they went,
until they came to an igloo.

It was the home of a small penguin.
He was reading a book.

The penguin said to Little Pig and his snow friend, "Tell me, do you know these words?"

And he showed them ***pig*** and ***together***.

"I am a ***pig***," said
Little Pig. "And
my snow friend
and I are ***together***.
What are you?"
And the penguin
told him he
was a ***penguin***.

"Which you do you like best?" asked Little Pig. "***Book***, ***wish***, ***change***, ***friend***, ***pig***, ***penguin***, or ***together***?"

“I like them all,” said Penguin.
“But best of all, I like ***together***.
That one lasts the longest.”

"I like that one best, too," said Little Pig and his snow friend, ***together*** .

FRIENDS TOGETHER SHOP

"And ***friend*** is an easy word after all," said Little Pig happily.